# SUPER TURBO ★

## vs. THE PENCIL POINTER

WRITTEN BY **EDGAR POWERS**
ILLUSTRATED BY **SALVATORE COSTANZA**
AT GLASS HOUSE GRAPHICS

LITTLE SIMON
NEW YORK   LONDON   TORONTO   SYDNEY   NEW DELHI

LITTLE SIMON
AN IMPRINT OF SIMON & SCHUSTER CHILDREN'S PUBLISHING DIVISION
1230 AVENUE OF THE AMERICAS, NEW YORK, NEW YORK 10020
FIRST LITTLE SIMON EDITION JUNE 2021 * COPYRIGHT © 2021 BY SIMON & SCHUSTER, INC. ALL RIGHTS RESERVED, INCLUDING THE RIGHT OF REPRODUCTION IN WHOLE OR IN PART IN ANY FORM. LITTLE SIMON IS A REGISTERED TRADEMARK OF SIMON & SCHUSTER, INC., AND ASSOCIATED COLOPHON IS A TRADEMARK OF SIMON & SCHUSTER, INC. FOR INFORMATION ABOUT SPECIAL DISCOUNTS FOR BULK PURCHASES, PLEASE CONTACT SIMON & SCHUSTER SPECIAL SALES AT 1-866-506-1949 OR BUSINESS@SIMONANDSCHUSTER.COM. THE SIMON & SCHUSTER SPEAKERS BUREAU CAN BRING AUTHORS TO YOUR LIVE EVENT. FOR MORE INFORMATION OR TO BOOK AN EVENT CONTACT THE SIMON & SCHUSTER SPEAKERS BUREAU AT 1-866-248-3049 OR VISIT OUR WEBSITE AT WWW.SIMONSPEAKERS.COM. DESIGNED BY NICHOLAS SCIACCA * ART SERVICES BY GLASS HOUSE GRAPHICS * ART AND COLOR BY SALVATORE COSTANZA * LETTERING BY GIOVANNI SPATARO/GRAFIMATED CARTOON * SUPERVISION BY SALVATORE DI MARCO/GRAFIMATED CARTOON * MANUFACTURED IN CHINA 0421 SCP * 2 4 6 8 10 9 7 5 3 1 * LIBRARY OF CONGRESS CATALOGING-IN-PUBLICATION DATA NAMES: POWERS, EDGAR J., AUTHOR. | GLASS HOUSE GRAPHICS, ILLUSTRATOR. TITLE: SUPER TURBO VS. THE PENCIL POINTER / BY EDGAR J. POWERS ; ILLUSTRATED BY GLASS HOUSE GRAPHICS. DESCRIPTION: FIRST LITTLE SIMON EDITION. | NEW YORK : LITTLE SIMON, 2021. | SERIES: SUPER TURBO, THE GRAPHIC NOVEL ; BOOK 3 | AUDIENCE: AGES 5-9 | AUDIENCE: GRADES K-4 | SUMMARY: "SUPER TURBO AND THE OTHER SUPERPETS FACE OFF AGAINST A MYSTERIOUS NEW FOE THAT SEEMS TO BE TRYING TO BURY TURBO ALIVE IN PENCIL SHAVINGS!"— PROVIDED BY PUBLISHER. IDENTIFIERS: LCCN 2020027925 (PRINT) | LCCN 2020027926 (EBOOK) | ISBN 9781534478381 (PAPERBACK) | ISBN 9781534478398 (HARDCOVER) | ISBN 9781534478404 (EBOOK) SUBJECTS: LCSH: GRAPHIC NOVELS. | CYAC: GRAPHIC NOVELS. | SUPERHEROES—FICTION. | HAMSTERS—FICTION. CLASSIFICATION: LCC PZ7.7.P7 SVP 2021 (PRINT) | LCC PZ7.7.P7 (EBOOK) | DDC 741.5/973—DC23 LC RECORD AVAILABLE AT HTTPS://LCCN.LOC.GOV/2020027925 LC EBOOK RECORD AVAILABLE AT HTTPS://LCCN.LOC.GOV/2020027926

# CONTENTS

IT WAS ALMOST THE *END* OF ANOTHER TYPICAL SCHOOL DAY.

**STUDENTS** ENJOYING THEIR FREE READING TIME? **TYPICAL.**

THEIR **TEACHER,** MS. BEASLEY, GRADING PAPERS? **TYPICAL.**

THE DESKS? CHALKBOARD? BOOKSHELVES? ALL **TYPICAL.**

EVERYTHING WAS COMPLETELY TYPICAL...**EXCEPT** FOR THIS GUY RIGHT HERE.

TURBO!
Official Classroom Pet
CLASSROOM C

TURBO MIGHT LOOK LIKE AN *ORDINARY* HAMSTER, BUT HE'S NOT! HE'S ALSO...

*SUPER TURBO*, THE MIGHTIEST SUPER-HAMSTER IN THE KNOWN UNIVERSE!

TURBO ISN'T THE ONLY CLASSROOM PET WITH A SUPERHERO SECRET IDENTITY! HE'S PART OF THE SUPERPET *SUPERHERO LEAGUE*.

NONE OF THE PETS AT SUNNYVIEW ARE TYPICAL, ORDINARY *CLASSROOM PETS*. BUT MORE ON THAT LATER...

BACK TO THIS TYPICAL SCHOOL DAY THAT'S ALMOST OVER.

DON'T FORGET TO REMIND THEM THAT THE SUPERPET SUPERHERO LEAGUE STUFF IS *TOP SECRET!*

TURBO ASKED ME TO LET YOU KNOW THAT HIS SECRET SUPERHERO *IDENTITY* IS TOP SECRET.

NONE OF THE STUDENTS AT SUNNYVIEW KNOW THAT THEIR CLASSROOM PETS ARE ACTUALLY *SUPERHEROES!*

YOU CAN *KEEP* A SECRET, RIGHT?

WAIT FOR IT...

RING-A-DING-DING!

THE SCHOOL DAY HAS OFFICIALLY ENDED.

SEE YOU TOMORROW, TURBO!

BYE, TURBO!

TURBO!
Official Classroom Pet
CLASSROOM C

MS. BEASLEY SPENT A FEW MINUTES GATHERING UP HER THINGS, AND THEN SHE LEFT TOO.

GOOD NIGHT, TURBO!

THERE WAS NO SUPERPET SUPERHERO LEAGUE MEETING SCHEDULED TONIGHT, WHICH MEANT TURBO COULD JUST TAKE IT EASY.

I MIGHT TAKE A *NAP.* OR...

I CAN CATCH UP ON MY *READING!*

BEHOLD, THE CLASSROOM C READING NOOK!

HMM, WHAT KIND OF STORY AM I IN THE MOOD FOR?

TURBO WAS JUST ABOUT TO BEGIN READING THE DETECTIVE STORY HE HAD CHOSEN WHEN *SUDDENLY*...

CREAK!

OH NO! SOMEONE'S COMING! I NEED A HIDING SPOT!

TURBO PEEKED OUT FROM UNDER HIS HIDING SPOT TO SEE WHO THE MYSTERIOUS *VISITOR* WAS.

THAT WAS CLOSE! BUT IT'S JUST THE *JANITOR*. NOTHING TO BE CONCERNED ABOUT!

UNLESS HE NOTICES MY CAGE IS *EMPTY!*

UH-OH! THE JANITOR IS STANDING RIGHT IN FRONT OF TURBO'S *CAGE!*

LUCKILY, THE TERRIBLE NOISE DIDN'T LAST FOR VERY LONG.

AFTER HE WAS FINISHED WITH WHATEVER HE WAS DOING, THE JANITOR PACKED UP HIS THINGS AND LEFT CLASSROOM C.

I THINK THE COAST IS CLEAR!

NOW TO *INVESTIGATE!*

TURBO LOOKED AROUND HIS CAGE.

NOTHING SEEMS TO BE *MISSING!*

MY EXERCISE WHEEL LOOKS THE *SAME.*

MY BED LOOKS THE *SAME.*

SPEAKING OF TURBO'S BED...

# CHAPTER 2

TURBO DIDN'T REALLY SLEEP WITH ONE EYE OPEN. HAMSTERS **CAN'T** DO THAT.

NOT EVEN *SUPERHERO* HAMSTERS!

JUST THEN, THE SCHOOL BELL *RANG*. THE SCHOOL DAY HAD OFFICIALLY BEGUN! WHICH MEANT...

RING-A-DING-DING!

THE STUDENTS WERE *ARRIVING!*

I'M SURE ONE OF THE STUDENTS WILL *NOTICE* WHATEVER IT IS THAT'S UP THERE.

BUT NONE OF THE STUDENTS SEEMED TO NOTICE.

HOW CAN THEY NOT NOTICE?

TURBO HAD BEEN KEEPING AN EYE ON MEREDITH. THE WORD IN THE SUPERPET SUPERHERO LEAGUE WAS THAT SHE WAS A POTENTIAL *TROUBLEMAKER*.

WHIRRRRRR!

POINTY!

SUDDENLY *EVERYONE* WANTED TO SHARPEN THEIR PENCILS.

WHIRRRRR!

STUDENTS SHARPENED
THEIR PENCILS *ALL DAY.*

WHIRRRRR!

THE *NOISE*
WAS TERRIBLE.

WHIRRRRR!

WHY IS EVERYONE SO *EXCITED* ABOUT A PENCIL SHARPENER?

BUT THE *SOUND* WASN'T EVEN THE *WORST* THING ABOUT THE NEW PENCIL SHARPENER...

TURBO WAS ABOUT TO *NOTICE*...

...THAT SOMETHING WAS *FALLING* INTO HIS CAGE.

WHIRRR!

IT WAS...

WHIRRR!

...PENCIL SHAVINGS!

SORRY TO *INTERRUPT*, SUPER TURBO, BUT MAYBE WE OUGHT TO *INTRODUCE* THE OTHER SUPERPETS FIRST?

GOOD IDEA!

THIS IS THE *GREAT GECKO,* ALSO KNOWN AS *LEO,* THE PET OF CLASSROOM A.

HE'S THE *OFFICIAL* CLASSROOM PET. PLEASE MAKE SURE TO MENTION THAT.

HERE IS *WONDER PIG.* SHE IS ALSO *OFFICIALLY* KNOWN AS *ANGELINA,* THE *OFFICIAL* CLASSROOM PET OF CLASSROOM B. DID I MENTION SHE'S *OFFICIAL?*

THAT WAS UNNECESSARY.

*CLEVER,* ALSO KNOWN AS THE *GREEN WINGER,* IS THE OFFICIAL CLASSROOM PET OF CLASSROOM D.

THE *FISH* IS NELL, ALSO KNOWN AS *FANTASTIC FISH.*

NELL LIVES IN A TANK IN THE HALLWAY, BUT SHE USES THE *TURBOMOBILE* TO GET AROUND ON OFFICIAL SUPERPET BUSINESS.

WARREN IS THE OFFICIAL PET OF THE SCIENCE LAB. HIS SUPERPET NAME IS *PROFESSOR TURTLE.*

THIS IS *FRANK*, ALSO KNOWN AS *BOSS BUNNY.* HE'S THE OFFICIAL PET OF THE PRINCIPAL'S OFFICE!

I KNOW THE PRINCIPAL'S OFFICE SOUNDS A LITTLE *SCARY*, BUT FRANK LIKES LIVING THERE. THE PRINCIPAL IS REALLY *NICE.*

SO NOW YOU KNOW ALL THE MEMBERS OF THE *SUPERPET SUPERHERO LEAGUE!* THESE ARE THE PETS THAT PROTECT SUNNYVIEW ELEMENTARY FROM *EVIL!*

AND SPEAKING OF EVIL, LET'S GET *BACK* TO THE *STORY!*

I WAS GOING TO REPORT STRANGE HAPPENINGS IN *MY* CLASSROOM TOO!

ME TOO!

STRANGE...HAPPENINGS? SOUNDS...MYSTERIOUS.

IN CASE YOU'RE WONDERING, PROFESSOR TURTLE TALKS *SLOW* BECAUSE...HE'S A *TURTLE.*

WHAT'S GOING ON?

LAST NIGHT, THE JANITOR CAME IN HERE AND INSTALLED SOMETHING. HE USED A *DRILL* AND IT WAS *LOUD!*

I COULDN'T SEE WHAT IT WAS AT FIRST BECAUSE I WAS SUPER TIRED AND I FELL ASLEEP.

BUT THE NEXT MORNING, THE *EVIL* REVEALED ITSELF.

THE EVIL IS...AN *ELECTRIC PENCIL SHARPENER!*

THE PENCIL SHARPENER... IS...*EVIL?*

NO, THAT'S NOT IT AT ALL! IT'S THE PENCIL *SHAVINGS* FROM THE PENCIL SHARPENER!

THE PENCIL SHAVINGS ARE FALLING INTO MY CAGE!

IF WE DON'T STOP THIS THING, IT'S GOING TO *BURY* ME ALIVE!

OF COURSE NOT! HE'S JUST A *PAWN!* THE REAL VILLAIN IS...

...THE PENCIL POINTER!

COME WITH ME. I NEED TO *SHOW* YOU SOMETHING.

# CHAPTER 4

THE SUPERPETS FOLLOWED
BOSS BUNNY THROUGH THE
VENT IN CLASSROOM C.

WHERE ARE WE GOING?

WE'RE HERE—THE PRINCIPAL'S OFFICE.

BEING A SUPERHERO, WONDER PIG HAS *SUPERSTRENGTH.*

WHICH COMES IN HANDY, BECAUSE VENT COVERS ARE *HEAVY!*

YESTERDAY THE PRINCIPAL HAD A MEETING WITH THE JANITOR.

THERE'S SOMETHING YOU NEED TO SEE.

GREAT GECKO, CAN YOU GET THE NOTEBOOK OFF THE PRINCIPAL'S DESK?

THE GREAT GECKO IS AN EXPERT CLIMBER.

HOW'S THAT FOR TEAMWORK?

ARE THOSE DRAWINGS OF YOU?

WHAT CAN I SAY? PRINCIPAL BRICKFORD IS A BIG *FAN* OF MINE.

BUT THAT'S NOT WHAT I WANTED TO SHOW YOU!

IT'S A *MAP!* THE CLASSROOMS ARE LABELED! AND IN EACH CLASSROOM...

...THERE IS AN X!

X MARKS THE SPOT!

OF THE PENCIL POINTER? GET IT?

THE PENCIL POINTER! HE PLANS TO *TAKE OVER* THE WHOLE SCHOOL!

BOSS BUNNY, YOU SOUND A LITTLE BIT LIKE OUR OLD *ENEMY* WHISKERFACE!

AS A REMINDER, *WHISKERFACE* IS THE HEAD OF THE *RAT PACK.* HE'S ALWAYS YELLING ABOUT TAKING OVER THE SCHOOL AND THEN THE WORLD.

HOW DOES INSTALLING A PENCIL SHARPENER IN EACH CLASSROOM HELP THE PENCIL POINTER TAKE OVER THE SCHOOL?

WELL, THE KIDS ARE MESMERIZED BY THE PENCIL SHARPENERS...

HE'S RIGHT! IS IT *MIND CONTROL?*

BUT WHO IS THE PENCIL *POINTER?*

MAYBE IT'S...PRINCIPAL... BRICKFORD?

NO WAY. PRINCIPAL BRICKFORD *LOVES* FRANK.

YEAH, AND I DON'T THINK IT'S THE JANITOR, EITHER. HE'S WAY TOO *NICE.*

WHO *HATES* CUTE, FUZZY, *ADORABLE* ANIMALS LIKE US?

WE SHOULD LOOK FOR MORE CLUES TO HELP US FIND OUT WHO THE PENCIL POINTER IS!

GOOD... IDEA...SUPER TURBO.

I FOUND SOMETHING!

CHAPTER 5

THE SUPERPETS RUSHED TO THE CAFETERIA TO LOOK FOR SNACKS...AND *CLUES!*

ON IT!

THE GREAT GECKO USED HIS SUPER CLIMBING SKILLS TO CLIMB THE SNACK CABINET.

BUT WHEN THE GREAT GECKO REACHED THE TOP...

GASP!

WHAT IS IT?

DID THE PENCIL POINTER STRIKE AGAIN?

GONE?!

WHERE DID THEY GO?

WE SHOULD SEARCH THE REST OF THE PANTRY!

NO SNACKS BEHIND THE CABINET!

THE SHELVES UP HERE ARE *EMPTY* TOO!

TURBO RECOGNIZED THAT *LAUGH.*

I RECOGNIZE THAT LAUGH!

SHOW YOURSELF, *WHISKERFACE!*

WH-WHAT DO YOU HAVE THERE?

SOMETHING WASN'T ADDING UP FOR SUPER TURBO.

WAIT!

I JUST REMEMBERED SOMETHING!

REMEMBER THE NOTE IN THE PRINCIPAL'S NOTEBOOK? *"TRIAL IN THE CAFETERIA"*?

YES... THAT WAS... MYSTERIOUS.

THE TRIAL THINGY IS WHAT WE CAME HERE TO INVESTIGATE.

WELL, AND TO GET SNACKS, TOO.

I AM TOO THE *PUNKY* POINTY! I DID ALL THAT EVIL STUFF!

YOU CAN'T EVEN SAY THE *NAME* RIGHT!

THE *REAL* PENCIL POINTER WANTED US TO RUN INTO WHISKERFACE IN THE CAFETERIA.

HE *PLANNED* THIS WHOLE THING TO DISTRACT US!

*GULP!*

# CHAPTER 7

THE SUPERPETS
HEADED **BACK TO**
CLASSROOM C.

TURBO HAD
NEVER SEEN HIS
FRIENDS SO *SAD.*

BACK INSIDE HIS CLASSROOM, TURBO LOOKED AT THE PENCIL SHARPENER.

IT ALMOST LOOKED LIKE IT WAS...*SMILING?*

YOU SEE IT, RIGHT? IT LOOKS LIKE IT'S SMILING!

ARE YOU *OKAY*, SUPER TURBO?

NO! THIS PENCIL POINTER IS MAKING ME *SO MAD!*

WHY CAN'T WE CATCH HIM?!

*WHO* IS THIS EVIL GENIUS? AND WHAT IS HIS EVIL *PLAN?*

I'M NOT GOING TO SIT AROUND AND WAIT FOR HIM TO BURY ME ALIVE IN PENCIL SHAVINGS!

NOW TO GET RID OF THIS THING, ONCE AND FOR ALL!

BUT THE PENCIL SHARPENER WAS *BOLTED* DOWN.

EVEN WONDER PIG'S SUPERSTRENGTH WASN'T ENOUGH TO *MOVE* IT.

YOU NEED... A *LEVER*.

A WHAT?

YOU NEED... A LEVER. TO... PRY...THE PENCIL SHARPENER... OFF!

HE'S RIGHT! MS. BEASLEY HAS A *RULER* ON HER DESK!

ON THE COUNT OF THREE!

# CHAPTER 8

WE SHOULD PROBABLY GO CHECK THE PENCIL SHARPENER TO MAKE SURE IT'S **NOT** BROKEN!

I HOPE WE DIDN'T BREAK IT!

IT'S STILL IN ONE PIECE!

ARE YOU GUYS READY TO GO TAKE CARE OF THE REST OF THEM?

CAN WE CLEAN UP IN HERE FIRST? WE MADE A **MESS.**

AS SUPER TURBO PICKED UP SOME LOOSE PAPERS, HE NOTICED *SOMETHING.*

IT'S A *DRAWING!*

OF *ME!*

HEY, LOOK! ONE OF THE STUDENTS DREW A PICTURE OF ME!

WOW, THAT'S REALLY GOOD!

SOMEONE WORKED REALLY HARD ON THAT PICTURE!

LOOK AT ALL THE DETAILS! THEY EVEN SHOWED HOW *FLUFFY* YOUR FUR IS!

IT WOULD TAKE A REALLY *POINTY PENCIL* TO DRAW ALL THAT DETAIL.

THAT'S WHEN TURBO *REALIZED* SOMETHING.

A REALLY *POINTY* PENCIL?

AND HE SUDDENLY FELT PRETTY *GUILTY.*

WHAT IF THIS WASN'T AN EVIL *PLOT* OF THE PENCIL POINTER? WHAT IF WE WERE *WRONG* THIS WHOLE TIME?

THE KIDS IN MY CLASS SURE LIKED SHARPENING THEIR PENCILS.

MY CLASS DID TOO.

TURBO REMEMBERED HOW *EXCITED* THE STUDENTS IN CLASSROOM C HAD BEEN ABOUT THEIR NEW PENCIL SHARPENER.

HE REALIZED HOW MUCH THE KIDS *LOVED* HAVING POINTY PENCILS.

ARE WE ALL IN AGREEMENT, THEN?

THE PENCIL SHARPENERS *AREN'T* EVIL.

NO ONE WANTS TO BURY US ALL IN PENCIL SHAVINGS.

WE KNOW WHAT WE NEED TO DO!

THE SUPERPETS DECIDED TO PUT THE PENCIL SHARPENER ON MS. BEASLEY'S DESK SO SHE WOULD SEE IT AS SOON AS SHE WALKED IN THE NEXT MORNING.

THEY EVEN REMEMBERED TO PUT HER RULER BACK WHERE IT BELONGED.

IT TOOK A LOT OF HARD WORK, BUT THE SUPERPETS *CLEANED* EVERYTHING UP AS BEST THEY COULD.

MS. BEASLEY WON'T KNOW WHAT HAPPENED TO THE PENCIL SHARPENER...

BUT SHE'LL NEVER SUSPECT THAT THE CLASSROOM PETS DID IT!

REMEMBER WHAT I SAID ABOUT THIS STUFF BEING TOP SECRET?

I THINK IT'S TIME FOR ALL OF US TO GO BACK TO OUR CLASSROOMS AND GET SOME REST.

YEAH, TODAY WAS REALLY EXHAUSTING!

I'M...EVEN... SLOWER... THAN...USUAL!

JUST ONE THING BEFORE I GO...

IF THE PENCIL POINTER ISN'T REAL...

...THEN WHAT'S THAT *MAP* WE FOUND?

AND WHAT DOES "TRIAL IN THE CAFETERIA" MEAN?

GOOD *QUESTIONS*, BOSS BUNNY.

I DON'T *KNOW* THE ANSWERS.

BUT I DO THINK WE WERE RIGHT TO LET THE STUDENTS KEEP THE PENCIL SHARPENERS.

TURBO CLIMBED INTO HIS CAGE, SETTLED INTO BED, AND FELL FAST *ASLEEP.*

MS. BEASLEY IMMEDIATELY NOTICED THE PENCIL SHARPENER ON HER DESK.

SHE COULDN'T FIGURE OUT WHAT IT WAS DOING THERE.

???

THEN MS. BEASLEY NOTICED *SOMETHING* ELSE.

SHE NOTICED THAT THE PENCIL *SHAVINGS* WERE *FALLING* INTO TURBO'S CAGE.

AWW, POOR TURBO.

SHE WENT TO GET THE JANITOR...

...TO HAVE HIM *REINSTALL* THE PENCIL SHARPENER...

...ON HER DESK. *FAR* AWAY FROM TURBO'S CAGE.

THE SOUND OF THE *DRILL* WOKE TURBO UP.

HE REALIZED HE WAS *SAFE* FROM THE PENCIL SHAVINGS!

ANOTHER SCHOOL DAY HAD OFFICIALLY *BEGUN.*

RING-A-DING-DING

GOOD MORNING, CLASS! I HAVE A FEW ANNOUNCEMENTS.

FIRST, WE WILL BE STARTING A TRIAL IN THE CAFETERIA TODAY...

AT THE MENTION OF A *TRIAL* IN THE CAFETERIA, TURBO'S EARS PERKED UP.

HE RUSHED TO THE EDGE OF HIS CAGE TO HEAR EVERY WORD OF WHAT MS. BEASLEY WAS GOING TO SAY.

WE'RE DOING A TRIAL RUN OF DELICIOUS *HEALTHY SNACKS* IN THE CAFETERIA.

YUMMY THINGS LIKE GLUTEN-FREE BREAD, FRESH FRUIT, AND YOGURT.

THE STUDENTS HAD A LOT OF QUESTIONS.

WILL WE STILL HAVE OUR OLD SNACKS?

YES, THESE HEALTHY SNACKS ARE *IN ADDITION* TO THE OTHER SNACKS.

THEN MS. BEASLEY TOLD THE STUDENTS ABOUT THE *NEW LOCATION* OF THE PENCIL SHARPENER AND WHY IT HAD BEEN MOVED.

I DISCOVERED THIS MORNING THAT THE PENCIL SHAVINGS WERE FALLING INTO TURBO'S CAGE...

THE STUDENTS OF CLASSROOM C WERE VERY CONCERNED ABOUT TURBO AND HAD A LOT OF QUESTIONS.

CAN'T GET ENOUGH OF THE
**SUPERPET SUPERHERO LEAGUE?**
CHECK OUT THEIR NEXT
ADVENTURE...

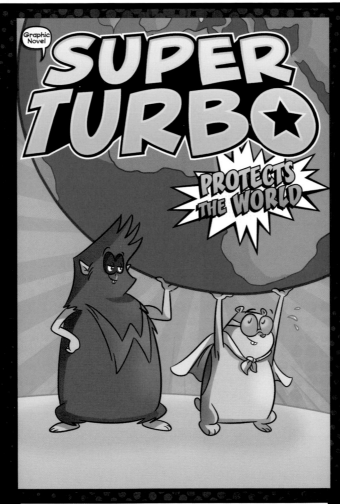

TURN THE PAGE FOR A SNEAK PEEK...